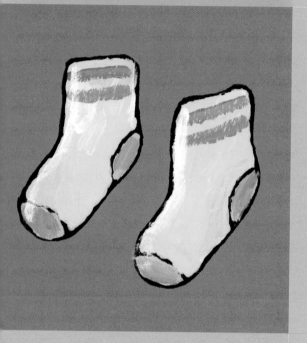

What does Ian play with at Grandma and Grandpa's?

Who lives with Grandma and Grandpa?

What does Ian take with him to Grandma and Grandpa's?

What makes the guest bed warm?

What does Ian eat and drink at Grandma and Grandpa's?

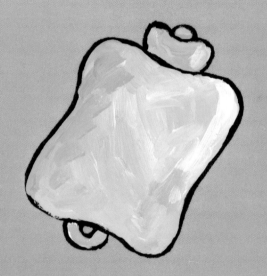

First published in Belgium and Holland by Clavis Uitgeverij, Hasselt – Amsterdam, 2011
Copyright © 2011, Clavis Uitgeverij

English translation from the Dutch by Clavis Publishing Inc. New York
Copyright © 2016 for the English language edition: Clavis Publishing Inc. New York

Visit us on the web at www.clavisbooks.com

Ian at Grandma and Grandpa's House written and illustrated by Pauline Oud
Original title: *Kas bij oma en opa*
Translated from the Dutch by Clavis Publishing

ISBN 978-1-60537-292-1

This book was printed in June 2016 at Publikum d.o.o., Slavka Rodica 6, Belgrade, Serbia

First Edition
10 9 8 7 6 5 4 3 2 1

Ian
at Grandma and Grandpa's House

Pauline Oud

Clavis
NEW YORK

Ian is going to stay at Grandma and Grandpa's house. Whoopee, that's really fun! Flap is coming with him. Ian puts his big picture book in his suitcase with the rest of his things. Now he is all ready to go.

Mommy takes Ian to Grandma and Grandpa's.
He carries his suitcase all by himself and Mommy carries
the flowers. Those are for Grandma and Grandpa.
"Hello Ian," Grandma and Grandpa call from a distance.
"So nice to have you visit!" And guess who appears behind
them? Curly the dog! "Hello Grandma and Grandpa,
hello Curly!" Ian says happily.

Soon after, Ian and Flap say goodbye to Mommy.

"See you tomorrow, dear Ian," Mommy says, and she gives him a big hug.

"Have fun at Grandma and Grandpa's!"

"I will," Ian nods.

"See you tomorrow!"

Ian and Flap wave goodbye to Mommy until she is just a little dot in the distance. Bye, Mommy!

Ian knows exactly where the guest bed is.
He runs right to it. "Wow, you brought a lot with you,"
Grandma says, astonished. "Did you come to live
with us?" "No!" Ian laughs. Silly Grandma!
"But it all fits on the bed." Grandma and Grandpa's
guest bed is really big. "It is a very special
bed," Grandma says mysteriously.
"You are going to sleep very well
in it, I am sure!"
Ian is sure too.

"Ian and Grandma, time for cake!"
comes a call from downstairs.
Ian gets a cup of juice and there is
cake for everyone.
Or not?

Curly sits next to Grandpa and looks hungrily at the table.

"No cake for Curly, Grandpa," Grandma says strictly.

"No, of course not," chuckles Grandpa and he winks at Ian, while he secretly slips Curly a piece of cake.

Silly Grandpa!

Yum! Curly likes the cake as much as Ian does.

After eating some cake, Grandpa and Ian take Curly to the park. Ian holds Curly firmly by the leash. When they are at the park, they let him run around freely. Grandpa tells Ian all about the trees and the plants and the birds in the park. Grandpa knows absolutely everything.

"Hey," says Ian
suddenly. "Where is Curly?"
Ian and Grandpa look behind the
trees and in the bushes. "Maybe he
lost his way?" Ian asks, frightened. "Well,
take a look in the pond," Grandpa says. Ian
sees the ducks in the water. And... what else
does he see? "Curly knows how to swim!" Ian
says cheerfully. Silly Curly!

"Ugh! Curly stinks!" Grandma says when Ian,
Curly and Grandpa come home. "Did you jump
into that dirty pond again?" she asks. "Come on, Ian.
We'll wash him clean," Grandma says.

Grandma and Ian wash Curly with dog shampoo.
"Mmm, now he smells good again," Ian says, pleased.
But, hey! Curly wags his tail and... what a splash!
Ian gets all wet!

"Now, Ian, will you come shopping with me?" Grandpa asks. "Grab your coat, and take the basket and a shovel."

"Go shopping with a shovel?" Ian asks, surprised. He's confused.

Ian runs into the garden after Grandpa and when Grandpa starts digging, Ian suddenly understands.
Of course!

At Grandma and Grandpa's,
vegetables like lettuce and tomatoes grow in
the garden. Ian and Grandpa pick out some
nice little carrots and some leeks. Ian helps
Grandpa dig with his own shovel. And
everything goes into the little basket.
"Look," Grandpa chuckles. "Curly is helping."
Curly digs deep in the mud with his paws.
"Now Curly is all dirty again!" Ian laughs.
Silly Curly!

Ian and Grandma make soup from the fresh vegetables.
"You can wash the carrots," Grandma says.
"There is still some dirt on them."
Ian scrubs with a brush until the carrots
are all nice and orange.
Granny cleans the leeks.
Mmm, it smells delicious in the kitchen!

When the soup is ready,
Grandpa makes his special pancakes.
They are special because they are so good
that you can't stop eating them.
That is probably because Grandpa
can throw the pancakes very high
up in the air. "Ooh," Ian calls.
"Higher!" Look, there is an
enormous stack on the table
already. Will Ian be able to
finish all those pancakes
by himself?

When Ian has eaten almost all the pancakes, it is time for bed. "Hey, the bed is already warm!" Ian says, surprised. "How is that possible?" "Yes, that is why it is such a special bed." Grandma winks, and she takes a hot water bottle from under the blankets.

'This bottle has heated the bed for you." Silly Grandma!

Ian gladly climbs into bed and Grandma starts to read
him a story. 'I'll keep reading until you've fallen asleep,'
Grandma promises.
Ian listens to the story with his eyes closed.
But then Grandma turns the page and... SHH...
Ian is asleep!

The next morning Mommy
comes to pick up Ian.
Ian tells her all about silly Curly,
the bath and shopping in the garden.
"And I slept very well," Ian says.
"Aha," Mommy says. "Then I know
what happened. You slept in the
warm bed!"

Ian grabs his little suitcase.
It's time to go home. "Bye Grandpa,
bye Grandma, bye Curly," Ian says.
Grandpa and Grandma wave goodbye.
"Will you come back to visit us soon?"
they ask. "I will!" Ian calls. "Woof, woof!"
Curly answers. Silly Curly!